THE
GOBLET
CRYING
FOR
WINE

The Goblet Crying for Wine

Fran Quinn

BLUE SOFA PRESS

Edited by Robert Bly

Published by Blue Sofa Press
Distributed by Ally Press, 524 Orleans Street,
Saint Paul, Minnesota 55104

ISBN: 09638722-1-4

The Goblet Crying for Wine is the second volume in a series from Blue Sofa Press: a cooperative effort, operated and funded by artists and writers. Blue Sofa was created to make available some of the work that has grown out of the Great Mother and New Father Conference, now in its twenty-first year.

ACKNOWLEDGMENTS
An earlier version of "In a Dusky Room" appeared in *Plainsong*. Earlier versions of "The Prepositions of You" and "A Story of Two Wives" were published in *Hopewell Review*. "Woodwinds" was published in *Walking Swiftly: Writings in Honor of Robert Bly*, ed. Thomas R. Smith (Ally Press, 1992). "Delano's Bar and Restaurant, Amherst, Mass., Good Friday, 1984, 1: 25 P.M." and "The Way They Meet" were published in *Painted Bride Quarterly*. "The Mystic in Spring" appeared in *Estero*. "The Way They Meet," "Love and the Working World," "Remembering Agamemnon in Tenant's Harbor, Maine," "Kansas," and "The Next Day" first appeared in *Milk of the Lioness*. "The Way They Meet" and "Resistance as a Prelude to This Poem" were published in *At the Edge of the Worlds*, lithographs by Janice Robert Forberg and poetry by Fran Quinn (Prasada Press, 1994).

to Diane with love

CONTENTS

THREE

ONE

Resistance as a Prelude to This Poem

At twilight the sun takes chances like this:
he jumps off the edge of the world,
penetrating the dark. He has nothing to lose.
He has spent all day with us.

So why not take chances now? Beneath the hand
that comes from under the past, why resist?
This mania of the middle way has, for centuries,
only encouraged the damned. We've buckled
        under the ideas
of those cautious men and women who have
        achieved
only *our* halting steps and doubts.

Bright star, close friend, at twilight
lead me, lead me with you
off the edge of the world.

The Mystic in Spring

for David Morris

When spring arrives, we start
looking for him. The woodpecker
begins knocking at the half-rotted
sycamore. The tulips peer up at the sky.
Even the roots spread out their hands.
Where is he? He must be here.
So much has happened that we didn't do.

The Next Day

The next day
no lover can find a place
where he can really be alone.
The woman sinks in
through the porous skin
until she's filled
all those places inside of him
with her dark hair and eyes. A hand
placed on his back last night
finds a way of reappearing
beneath his palm
in the form of a gesture
only she uses.
A voice counterpointing his own
gives tongue to experiences he had
when he was a girl, before manhood
balanced its uneasy weight
upon his shoulders. If he's lonely today
it's because
her voice is calling
to be reunited with her body again.

Remembering Agamemnon
in Tenant's Harbor, Maine

Sometimes poems rise up like the sea
to batter our coastline. A single word
hollows itself like an old Taoist. It repeats
far out from land.
We go for our ships.

The sea grows calm
when the bow touches water. For weeks
nothing happens
but that sound
coming in
from out there.

        We stare
at the mirroring water.
What would you sacrifice
to set sail?

Dandelion

for Joanne Charbonneau

In the dark cave we used to call
home, lie the bones of our former life. There

crinoline crackles like static electricity
and the young boy at the prom door

waits as awkwardly as the flowers he holds.
It was then night held its breath

til its face turned green. Some things
are cut off exactly when they're

most beautiful. As dawn came
it blew us past college and travel,

past marriage
and knowing and we're

flying still just barely
above the ground

like the white seed
in springtime.

An Adolescent Boy
Thinks of Women

for Mark Clements

How hard it is even to
approach one. And to hold
her hand, or cup her face
and say something tender,

that would be impossible.
So I'll be playful and tough
and give her an orange
knowing secretly it is myself.

I know the rind protects
me but still I hope she will with
her right hand, lift my outer
skin and slowly tear it away, saying,

"Shining boy! Sweet
one! Burn my lips!"

Love and the Working World

for Stan Haney

I

When I've spent time with this woman
my body fills with
trees and wild animals. The desert spots

are green again. The small tracks
her mouth made
form themselves into

amulets and pendants
absorbed by the skin. Why,
I am lucky all week!

As I walk, my muscles
plink against my veins
like a kalimba.

II

I cannot resist singing
to the man who hired me.
He too knows
the music of his body
rises when he goes home.

I caught him once
dancing in his office
just before closing time.

Small Love Poem

Have you seen, at dockside,
two boats jostling against each other?
The waves say it's playful love.
Safe in the harbor, they have
made a home where nuzzling
each other in public

opens everyone's heart. If you notice
at sunrise and sunset, you need
no money; everything, but everything,
is gold; and you know you wouldn't
spend a cent of it, even if you could.

Diner Coffee

for B. Eugene McCarthy

I walk in groggy, hating the world,
blinded by eye-level sun,
trying to shake off my lack of sleep
and the shards of dreams that jut from my brain
and are pissed off at me because I pay no
   attention,

and there she is, pure Italian angel,
hair cascading like a memory of last night's
disarray, and dispensing
black energy into half-washed mugs.
I join the rest, lean into the counter.

We trust this mug of coffee like the bitter facts of
   layoffs
and homelessness and addictions. We hold it
and know that we'll vote for what
we already have, no matter
how bad it is.

She comes back again. I order
the usual: two eggs, over easy, bacon homefries and
wheat toast, thinking, "Wheat toast
is a change for the better." She pours a refill
and I stare into the cup.

Deep down
the earth is hot and liquid
and way out
we're spinning through
the universe.

Early June Child

for Jonathan Blunk

We forgot
that green
was our favorite.

Like the bad
child, green
had run away
and throughout

all the white and desperate
months, our hearts, searching
for what we worked
so hard

to bring to the world,
to nurse
through the heat and hard
times, almost stopped

believing. Now
he has returned,
frightened
by how much dark

is still out there, and we
don't know how
to cover up

our grief, our
anger, our joy.

January at the Door

Bleak and uncanny fields!
Homeland of the poor.
Under the skirts of night
the uneasy heart of the year

pumps through the hours and days
with only a dusting of snow
in a landscape that hasn't had rain
in weeks, and maybe in months.

The widow sits near the stove.
Two roses arrive at the door
with no card or message enclosed.

The gift is startlingly pure:
a promise and memory of love
when the body is ready to go.

Why They Told Us What They Have

So it's spring again
and we're *supposed*
to be happy.
We've been trained to it.
It's demanded of us.

The trees flash their buds, quickly spreading
their petals . . . baring their hearts,
ripping themselves open
with odor, pushing out,
pushing out, and then
tossing themselves into the
wind, onto the ground
with pleasure, they tell us,
with pleasure,

making way
for the leaves
that stay and stay,
a repetition, a
redundancy
of green
all summer long,
all summer
long.

The Way They Meet

The traveller alone on the road
as night ascends through the trees.
He looks intently at the shapes
as they fade. The other night
comes down and the landscape is gone.
His feet, his only guide, the toes
blunted by his shoes.

Beyond his vision, a woman cries
in a lighted room. Her hair
blond and tightly curled. "Excuse me,"
she says. The hand she moves toward her face
never touches it. "The river is frozen . . .
and nothing will happen here."

She cannot see the way the light
softens the table's edge.
She feels a beauty in entrapment
where the wild remains wild
but does not move.
"Excuse me," she says.

The traveller
still on the road
walks slowly,
a tight curl of light in his mind.

Composition in Blue for Kim
and the Imagination

There is a bird in that oak
just to the left of that blue house.
If you cannot see it, it is because
the bird is blue and if one could
characterize the little song it sings
one would have to hear that it *is* blue,
so blue one could mistake it for the bird.

Now certainly on its branch
the bird should be so clearly seen
that one would have to be blind to miss it,
especially when it is blue; but, no, my dear,
for notice how late into fall it is and
this sunny day distracts our attention,
so we see the sky and not the bird. And

part of me is so happy that I'm willing to say,
"It is the sky I hear singing that insistent
little song." And if I said that (which I did),
it is certainly as true as that other set of facts.
For the bird arrived here as much at my bidding
as by its own will; just as you would be
speaking to me now if I gave you a chance.

And if you are to insist that you are not
here in my office it is only because you wish to
    confuse
the reader who is no more in my office than you
but could only tell so when you drew his (I'm
    wrong)
her attention to it. So give me your hand, the right
    one,
for in travelling this way, we could fly almost
    anywhere
and move to such distances that everything would
    turn blue.

Worcester in Sunlight and Darkness

for Ann Neelon

When I look around in sunlight
I do not see the city that I knew
when you and I walked about
talking of poetry, or loosened our morals
to let in the world we did not know.

Yet I still see your face
in the garden at dusk
surrounded by tiger lilies,
and wild blue chickory. The tiger lilies,
closing at the end of the day,
still leave a place for you to kneel.

Once in mid-afternoon
we started talking near Green Island
and continued walking, talking
till our faces had no light,
a melancholy trick
the world played on us.

But the world
cannot get dark enough
to blot you out;

and distance fails;

and so does sun and time.

Nothing is gone that I know of
that's in me,
and nothing that I know of
that is you.

TWO

Delano's Bar and Restaurant, Amherst, Mass., Good Friday, 1984, 1:25 p.m.

They always leave it . . .
that small circle of wine
in the bottom of the glass

as if there's something
down there they can't take in.
The dregs, they call it; the bottom
is what's there . . .

the finish, the
end. It's yours
when you take it
all in.

My father greeted death this way:
he waited until we were alone,
his last words long gone,
five or six days of pure silence,

four tears,
then a smile,
but nothing left —
no little circle,

the glass
handed to me
clean.

A Story of Two Wives

I

Let me tell you a story. Because then the dead
will be brought back to us, because then we
will be brought back to ourselves as a piece of the
    future.
As I rise from the table to reach for some bread
I feel my hands grow old and suddenly I am

my grandmother, brushing her hair from her fore-
    head, her apron
wet along the navel line from leaning on the sink,
    the smoke
rising behind her at the table. My grandfather's pipe
lit half for reverie and half for love of all in his past

and his present. When his first wife died she
made him promise, right there, seated beside her on
    the bed,
she made him promise: "Paddy, you're still young
and I know you'll get married again, but promise me,
promise me you'll be buried with me." Such devotion!

II

I am here leaning on this table, bread cut,
wondering what else
I need and where I put it, as if I already had it.
She, the second wife,
seated with him on the divan in the front room,
quiet and warm together.

He looked at her. "Minnie," he said to her,
"Minnie, you know,
I have to be buried with Patricia."
The chill entered.

I saw the shadow also enter that afternoon,
reminding me
that it was more than dusk crossing over the lion
    claws
clamped on the glass
balls at the bottom of the piano stool.

III

He slept his last few nights on that divan and every
    hour
he would call to her saying, "Minnie,
you must make sure I am buried with Patricia!"
He looked at me:
"I don't believe she'll do it."

Two days before he died
she came out of her bedroom holding some papers:
"It's a three-grave lot."
She lived alone nearly twelve years.

When she was dying she held me back,
tugging at my sleeve as I left the room.
She drew my ear close to her mouth, "Do you think
    they've been
alone long enough by now?" she whispered.

She had them dig the grave so she could lie the way
    she always had,
between them both,
not an intrusion, but a place where past and future
    meet
as in a story
of someone leaning on a table reaching for bread.

The Importance of Gargoyles

Tonight I rehearse some words for my mother's life
to free us both, as in the old days when men carved
gargoyles in wood or stone to give form to their fears,
to catch them and stop them from roaming in the
    world.

Without these words my sister has been caught by
something she can't name; and my son has been left
unborn and when he does arrive he
won't have a clue why he's so lonely.

While making love to his wife
he will pass through his sperm
something like a shadow only bigger, heavier.

Woodwinds

for Robert Bly

The woodwinds have a voice
　　　　that's clear and low,
a reminder of melancholy, or

my mother's aging hand
　　　　smoothing my
brow into its mortality.

Dust gathers on the books,
　　　　wisdom untouched
for so long. The blind poet

is ready to sing again
　　　　at anyone's
scanning eye or touch,

but the new book lies proud
　　　　and bold, brassy
red cover, only half finished.

So many I love have died
　　　　and will die.
Her hand, her kindness

do not compete with those
        of my lover.
Both have their separate graces,

both have their own time.
        A sound clear
and calm, a sound low and

lusty. The sun breaks across
        the old book and
the new. I can hear both voices

reach their crescendo together.
        Listen for a time,
this time, this music. Now

one begins to fade. The woodwinds
        have a voice that's clear
and low, a reminder of melancholy.

Kansas

Kansas lies down
because the rest of the country
won't. It rolls on one side
then the other,
verdant or brown. Here
the earth speaks only
to the earth. When people came
they were told to rest
or else continue on.

Because Kansas knows the value
of sleep, night hangs
just above the waist,
and in daytime the sky
rests on any hand
held up to it.

Indiana Surface Watching

Here where the forest runs thin
and the plains have not begun
the land rises and falls like easy breathing.
Each town repeats the pattern of the town before
like a truth they told us when we were young.
It seems so easy to plan; it's all been laid out.
Cows and hogs, in their stupid way, look quite smart
out here. They know the land which no one knows
ten miles from Harvard Square. They eat the grass
and sink their hooves an inch or two in earth
content to know they plan to stay. A bird, no, two,
have settled in a tree. They're out of sight.
They do not sing but talk the way a jay or crow does.
"Here we are," they say. "We seem to fit."

Laurel Elizabeth Crying at Her Baptism on a Hot July Day

Here in this heat
we want to be held
    and held apart
and cry because the contradiction's
    unresolved
once we are lovers
    on these shores.

And we are lovers
    immediately
when we are born;
    our open arms
reach out to anyone
    we cannot know.

We have our body's water
    and its salt
the sun draws out of us
    on any summer day
and every child outside the womb
    is bathed in that.

Without Simile There Can Be No Joy
Three Views as Spring Arrives on Campus

I

There is nothing discreet
about the flowers
that bask and seduce like coeds in the sun
all summer long, or the birds
bursting from tree to tree, battling it out
or tumbling like athletes
                                    and the dogs
their tails up, proud of their genitals:
they display them like awards or
scholarships long fought for and
received with much pomp and circumstance.

II

Or is it the other way: the flowers
blushing at our display, the birds
trying to escape our violence, our
ignorance, and only the dogs brazen enough
to lift their tails yipping, "Kiss
this, you fools!"?

III

Some say
the birds,
the flowers,
the dogs
don't care
at all.

What moves
them is
the sun
rising hotter
every day.

The coeds?
The athletes?
The scholars
and prize winners
display
what they can.

They are like
shadows that
stretch west
in the morning
and east
in the afternoon

awaiting the grave
where the light
appears briefly
then is snuffed out.

Early Morning Tea

for Jim Watt and Lee Verner

This morning there is
something in the air like
silence or autumn.

The body languishes
in its memory
of sleep, so I choose

tea. It comes with chimes
and its darkness says,
"You have friends on the

Great Plains that can sleep
another hour or two."
It says, "There's a chance

to hover above the world."
Tea offers a mystery
we can fathom all

the way down to the
bottom. It teaches us
to walk with no effort,

i

to face north with no
fear, to rise only as high
as our neighbors and to

gratefully return the tools
we borrowed yesterday.

An Alchemy of Intercourse

for Mark McCarthy and Mary Laurel True

As in the old days the red gowned men
and the red gowned women
meet in the hall, swelling
the chamber walls. And the white gowned
men and the white gowned
women rush
through the dark corridors
like light along tubing. Then
in the salty air they made,
someone sacred appears, so small
the dill seed seems larger than cathedrals
and all the holy cities of the earth
empty, as a blush
falls across the world.

Sinner

Some days I love people so much
I do almost anything to stay with them.
They can say what they want
and I agree
and even add to their arguments
in ways I don't believe at all.

To sit there and just look at them —
their noses, their hands, their eyes
expressing what they will
and I, a devotee, a penitent
who has sinned by disagreeing with them
on other days, by dismissing what they stood for
when I knew less than they
but better.

Home again and alone, I've confessed
my lust, my inattention
to truth, my greed
for company, my adoration
of their god. Forgiven
I have sinned again.

THREE

Mangoes

Together
we say "parting;"
you draw your comb through your hair.

The bright orange, the morning,
the large flat pit of the
mango, sweet flesh
opening. The tongue
can't believe the
memories it has.

Again "parting"
I say, but you're not
listening.

We are what's left of
wholeness, and the juice
what's left of the long night
laughing together.
Again and again the pit
streaming long yellow hair. I

can't let
that much go.
The old skin

now off.
"Parting." "Parting."
Said like some
nourishment.
The sun wants you
for himself

in work, in adventure,
in his slow luxurious
travels toward the west.

The Prepositions
of You

So I speak
of you when
I do not speak
to you and
the words I choose
are marked by
the imprint you
made when your tongue
swirled around mine
or your breath,
soft-gloved and pure,
reached beyond
the uvula to the
voice box and my
breath compressed
against lung walls can find
no way out except
past you or through you;
and even after you
remove to a distant
outer place, all I say
and breathe
seek out that place

if not in body and time
then in symbol.
Pierced by the minute hand
and the hour hand the words
hang onto each other
longing to form
new vows in you.

Economy: A Love Poem

No credit,
no credit at all
to my massive love.

I am so spent
that I can
barely, just
barely
move.
The wallet

shakes out
dust. My dust!
What value is
this? What hope
if tomorrow or
what's left

of today, costs
anything?
Your eyes and
something,
something
you haven't

said, fills me
with wonder . . .
but again
your eyes
with their
deeper

understanding
of blue.
Oh, the sun!
The sun is
scattered
by this

deep green
feathering
of leaves.
No credit,
no credit at all
to my massive love.

In March

for Grace Farrell

All winter the brook
has had nothing to say.
Now it says it so fast
we can't understand. What
did it see at its source
that caused it to run
so wildly?
                    It has
drowned all the sheep
in the meadow and washed
the shed off its pilings.

As You: An Autobiography

A raccoon, dead, on its back
at the edge of the road, front paws
spread out, and hind paws too,
as if in sexual
ecstasy death
came and took him. He didn't care.

I know sometimes I too have felt,
lying next to or under
you, I was
so full, death
could have his way:
how you matched me

so perfectly, how it wasn't
me I felt anymore. I was already
dead, gone to another world (maybe to you . . .
     or maybe
just gone). I couldn't remember
my life and I
didn't care to.

After the Dark Wind

I grew old
only after the dark wind came.
Now I've no desire
for anything but you.
The silver blades of your eyes
flash blue light.
Bury them in my chest.
My knees already buckled
when you entered. I kneel,
I kneel until you bid me rise.

Against the Blue Wall

Have you heard the singer in the garden
responding to the trumpet vine? Each note
wants to perfume the air.

Look at the grapes shaking like maracas. Their seeds
are so precious that women from this town
carry grapes between their breasts
and the breasts themselves seem like huge
clusters beaded with sweat.

I look past your blond hair and find our shadows
glimmering light against the blue wall.

The Slow Man Discovers Love
in the Corridors

for Diane Prenatt

There you were, standing among
the pungent odors of coffees, among the
bright yellow pencils, among the grades
and the blue books. Like light you
filled the corridors, soaking the midwinter skies.

I saw right away love was
endangered, so
I took you in, the way a child does
on a summer night, inhaling among
the scents of sleep and jasmine.

Carpet and Shadow: An Illicit Affair

Her eyes narrowed down to a single ray
so fine that it slipped through the center of his eye
and pierced a thought. Finally, all he could do
was adjust his seat so he could see her better
if he looked up again, which he didn't.

His uneasiness betrayed the fact he would be unable
to act for himself. His glance
now slid from left to right
over the yellow carpet roses, over the rigid leaf edges.

He tried to concentrate on the roses
but the shadow galloped out of the carpet,
over the leaves and roses and hid just under
the thin heel of her shoe with its own
complementary shadow. She tripped
when she rose and he reached for her.

Looking for the Large

for Ann Igoe

We were reckoning. And there were
answers floating like dust motes
all around us.

We were thinking and thinking,
expecting the problems to be
solved

by a mountain, or the sky or some
heavy heeled god that could crush
everything we hated.

We were reckoning. And there were
answers floating like dust motes
all around us.

In a Dusky Room

I have seen in the tips of the apple blossoms
a snow so cold it won't go away.

I have seen in the bark of the elm blight upon blight
until the entire tree toppled.

I have held you in a dusky room
and seen your shadow rise and be gone.

I have seen in your eyes an absence so huge
light cannot reach it.

I have felt the perfect ring of your body
that you slipped on my finger go dry

and an emptiness entered me
as if I were the center of our wedding band.

Along the curve of your curling hair
a small coffin is being carried down.

Now my heart is convinced
all circles, by nature, are empty.

So I must kneel down and pray
for the wings to appear

and the presence of one that I love.

The Way Things Work
at the Forge

for Ed Shaughnessy

The hammer hitting
against the metal
makes it thin.
The sparks
are flying
and specks of gold
are flying with them.

The color of the air
changes imperceptibly.
The hammer
hits again,
the rhythm set
like the heart
beat it is.

We hunger
for what
will be made.
It's rough work
and it's
violent, but
we want it.

Sometimes we confuse ourselves
by saying, "We need it."
But "desire" is already
a goal achieved and
"lust" develops a halo, or
at least an aura.

We don priestly robes packing
our bags like missionaries. We are here for
conversion. We are here
to find the wounded leper who
licks his own sores and to praise
what we were taught to hate.

The hammer hits
again and again,
the harsh music
changing slowly
into chimes as the
goblet's mouth
widens, clearly crying,
crying for wine.

ABOUT THE AUTHOR

FRAN QUINN was born in Easthampton, Mass., May 5, 1942. He is presently Poet-in-Residence at Butler University in Indianapolis. He has served as editor of *GOB* and *The Worcester Review* and has produced weekly book review and poetry shows for radio. Mr. Quinn has taught at Assumption College, the College of the Holy Cross, Worcester Polytechnic Institute, Clark University, Worcester State College, Rivier College, Northeastern University, St. John Preparatory School (Shrewsbury) and St. Charles Academy (Woonsocket). He has also worked as a janitor, police dispatcher, bag boy, veterinary anesthesiologist, and bookmobile driver for the Westborough, Mass. town library. He has previously published *Milk of the Lioness* and (with Janice R. Forberg) *At the Edge of the Worlds*. He won the Hopewell Prize in 1992. He has read widely across the United States and Canada.

NOTE FROM THE AUTHOR

I would like to thank Michael True, both teacher and friend to me; Susan Neville and Geoffrey Bannister, who believed enough in me to give me a job; Ann Igoe, Jim Watt, Mary Fell, David Williams, and Lou Camp, my early critics; Sarah Bennett, for her care in designing this book; Gay and Stuart Schecter for theirs in printing it; and most especially Robert Bly, who not only believed in the manuscript but helped to organize, edit and advise throughout the entire process of getting these poems into book form.

Designed by Sarah Bennett in
Leicester, Massachusetts. Prin
ted on Sundance Natural 70#
vellum by Stuart and Gay
Schecter at Point
Reyes Printing,
Point Reyes,
Ca
li
fo
rn
ia.
The typeface is Sabon.